T0198909

My Name is Charlie

Story by A.E. Keener

Illustrated by Susan Anderson-Shorter

AuthorHouse™
1663 Liberty Drive
Bloomington, IN 47403
www.authorhouse.com
Phone: 833-262-8899

Because of the dynamic nature of the Internet, any web addresses or links contained in this book may have changed since publication and may no longer be valid. The views expressed in this work are solely those of the author and do not necessarily reflect the views of the publisher, and the publisher hereby disclaims any responsibility for them.

This book is printed on acid-free paper.

ISBN: 978-1-4490-7576-7 (sc)
ISBN: 978-1-4685-9013-5 (e)

Library of Congress Control Number: 2010900500

Print information available on the last page.

Published by AuthorHouse 04/05/2021

authorHOUSE®

Dedication

This story began as a writing prompt for a class. I was supposed to write about a dog facing euthanasia. Being the animal lover that I am, I found it hard to pick up my pen and write; however, I am glad that I did.

For you see, Charlie became more than just a character to me. Charlie became a voice, a figure, of those animals that have to face each new day hoping for someone to take them home. With all our own worries and problems in life, we often forget that animals face problems, too. What do they do when they have no home to go to? What do they do when there is no food in their bowls? What do they do when people pass by and hardly acknowledge that they exist?

So, this story is dedicated to all the animals that are still waiting for a loving home. Since they cannot speak, Charlie will speak for them.

Part of the proceeds from the sale of this book
is donated to non-kill animal shelters.

What is this place? It's smelly, cold, and foreign. The ground is hard, and iron bars prevent me from leaving my four-foot square. The dogs, they bark and whine all the time, never ceasing; their howls filled with need, fear, and loneliness. This isn't my home. My home is warm, soft, and filled with people.

Why am I here? Did I do something wrong? Was it because I refused to take a bath? If that's true, I promise I'll be good. When you say, "Charlie, time for your bath," I'll jump right in with my tail wagging.

A Cage...that's what I'm in, both physically and mentally. I want to roam free and explore new scents. I want to chase that stupid squirrel that lives in the tree in my yard.

Oh, there are scents and creatures to keep my mind occupied. The overwhelming stench fills my nose to the point of numbness. And also, there's this other smell. It comes from the white double doors down the hall. It is unfamiliar to me. It reminded me of the smell from the bird the neighbor's cat left on our front step. That smell...I don't like it. It is so foreign and unfamiliar that I fear it.

Besides the smells, there are also the rats. They creep through the bars to eat some of my food. Unlike squirrels, they don't like it when you play with them. My paw is still sore from the other day when I tried to chase a rat.

Why am I here? What did I do wrong? I sit, I beg, I speak, and roll over. Was it because I wasn't a good guard dog? Did you not like me lying around in the sun so much? If that's true, then next time I'll be on guard twenty-four/seven.

People occasionally come to visit the other dogs and me. I don't recognize any of them. Some of the people are friendly, like the little girl who took the Chihuahua in the adjoining cage home with her.

And then, there are the people in the white coats. They are completely emotionless and reek with that unfamiliar smell. They come periodically and select a certain dog that they take through the white doors. The dog that is chosen is scared and shaking badly. Because, we all know that the dog that goes through those doors is never seen or heard from again.

Why am I here? What did I do wrong? I bark and wag my tail. Was it because I didn't want to go to the vet? If that's true, then I promise the next time I'll go willingly.

One of those men is at my cage. He glances at me, then at his clipboard. He opens the cage and drags me out. I am a quivering mass as he carries me through the white doors.

The doors lead to a room. It is so white that it hurts my eyes. The man places me on a counter in the center of the room. Pointed objects line the tables, and I am engulfed in that unfamiliar smell.

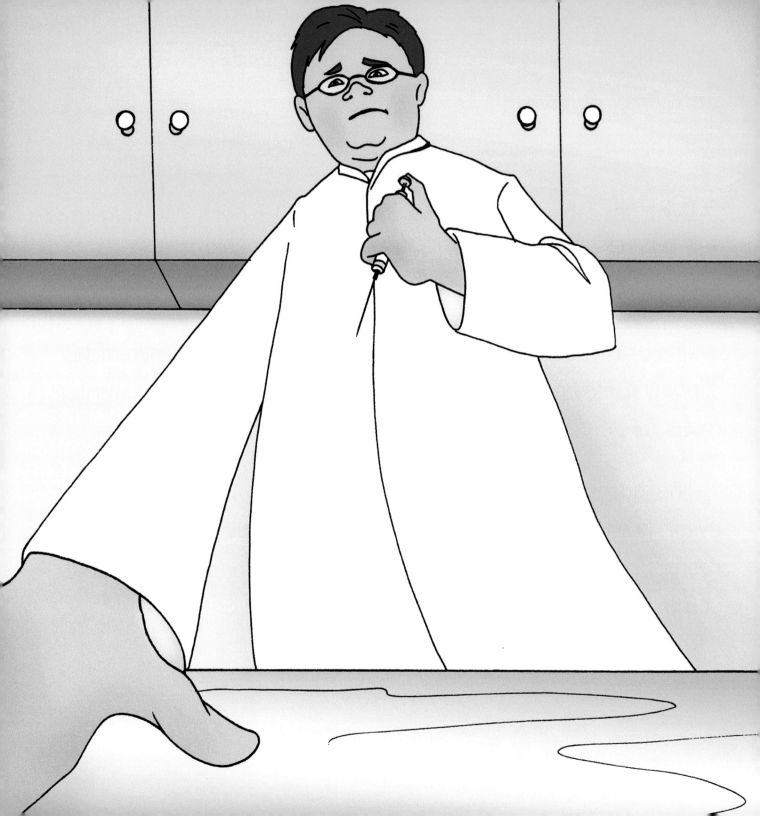

The man sets down his clipboard and picks up one of those pointed objects. He attaches a vial with a strange milky-white liquid in it. Am I getting a shot? Is that all my family wanted me to do, get a shot? I wag my tail. Maybe I will finally go home.

Grim-faced, the man turns to me. He places the needle against my shoulder as I wait patiently. Though he shows no emotion, I sense an air of nervousness surrounding him. I lick his hand to reassure him. I know it will be all over in a moment.

Just as he is about to administer the shot, the lady from the front desk runs in yelling "stop!" The two talk for a moment before she picks me up and takes me out of the room. As we walk by the other dogs, they bark in confusion. I am just as confused as they are since no dog has ever returned once it goes through the white doors. Instead of stopping at my cage, we continue to the front of the building. There, watching me as we walk in is the little girl who took the Chihuahua. The girl tugs her mother's sleeve and says, "I want that one, Mommy!"

My name is Charlie. I can sit, beg, and roll over. I don't like baths, but I'll still take them. I'm a good dog. At least, that's what my new family tells me.